NORTHERN ENGLAND

Edited By Megan Roberts

First published in Great Britain in 2018 by:

Young Writers
Remus House
Coltsfoot Drive
Peterborough
PE2 9BF
Telephone: 01733 890066
Website: www.youngwriters.co.uk

Book Design by Spencer Hart

SB ISBN 978-1-78896-969-7
Printed and bound in the UK by BookPrintingUK
Website: www.bookprintinguk.com
YB0381P

FOREWORD

Young Writers was created in 1991 with the express purpose of promoting and encouraging creative writing. Each competition we create is tailored to the relevant age group, hopefully giving each pupil the inspiration and incentive to create their own piece of work, whether it's a poem or a short story. We truly believe that seeing their work in print gives pupils a sense of achievement and pride in their work and themselves.

For Stranger Sagas, we challenged secondary school pupils to write a mini saga – a story in just 100 words. They were given the choice of eight story starters to give their imaginations a kick-start:

- Today, I hired someone to solve my murder...
- Don't go in the woods, they told me...
- I looked around, desperately searching for an escape...
- "Tell me everything you know, child..."
- My torch flickered and went out. I was alone in the darkness...
- I knew there would be consequences, but I did it anyway...
- *Please let this be a dream*, I thought...
- "You can save only one," the voice said...

They could use any one of these to begin their story, or alternatively they could choose to go it alone and create that all important first line themselves. With bizarre beginnings, mysterious middles and enigmatic endings, the resulting tales in this collection cover a range of genres and showcase the talent of the next generation. From fun to frightening to the weird and wonderful, these mini sagas are sure to keep you entertained and take you to strange new worlds.

CONTENTS

THE MINI SAGAS

The Bang

"There they are! Get them!"
"Run!" exclaimed Lizzy.
As fast as ever, the girl ran past the science room, past the lunch hall, jumped over the wall and away from the killers.
"Who... Who was that?" puffed Amy, trying to catch her breath.
"I don't know, but they shouldn't be here!" whispered Lizzy.
After sneakily getting back to class, the girls rushed to the teacher and explained everything.
"Are you certain it wasn't a student?" questioned the teacher.
"Positive!" they both said.
Bang! Bang!
"What was that?" asked Lizzy.
"Lizzy!"
Bang!
"*No!* She's gone... dead!"
"No! Amy! *No!*"

Tara Horn (12)

Consequences

Farmer Ray from Iowa set out to build a baseball park. He was gambling everything, not just his life, but the lives of his wife and daughter. He knew what he was doing. He knew it was the right decision for those who had been forgotten. They were former legends, but no one knew their names, unfairly accused of taking bribes to throw a game. Their reputation of being dishonest had no chance of redemption. Ray knew that he had to take a risk after hearing their voices one evening. He knew there would be consequences...

Abbey Hazel Rose Steel (14)
Communicate Tutoring, Carlisle

The Stranger Awaits

My torch flickered and went out. My blood curdled, *it* was coming closer. As I staggered on my trembling legs, a knife, flying faster than a bullet, pierced the air. It missed my eye by an inch. Craving freedom, my hopeless body crawled towards the scraped oak door. *It*, with its slimy fingers and villainous, malicious claws, grabbed my ankle. Its gruesome nails slowly injected dark toxins into my leg. Then I heard an ear-piercing, horrifying and unnerving shriek, only to realise that it was the terror-struck voice of my own. That sound... *the stranger awaits...*

Amaan Kauji (12)

Eden Boys' School Preston, Preston

The Hero Next Door!

"You can save only one," the mysterious voice screeched.
The boy shouted, "I will save as many as I can!"
"Are you sure you're making the right choice?" the mysterious voice answered.
The boy was terrified but he didn't want to show his emotions. He needed to wake up and become the hero he was born to be. He didn't know he needed to show everyone his secret talents. A mysterious voice couldn't pull him away from his destiny. Unfortunately, his parents passed away in a car accident. He was a boy with a lion's heart...

Mikaaeel Hussain (15)
Eden Boys' School Preston, Preston

Don't Go In The Woods

Desperately searching for an escape, fighting through overgrowth, had I really just come here because of a stupid letter I'd found? *Come help, I'm in the forest. Tom.*
Glaring around, I could just about make out the vile creature staring me in the eye. It looked like death. Suddenly, I found myself pacing. I felt as though it was the end of me. Tom was dead, what made me come here? My life flashed before my eyes. I should've listened to them. The creature leapt, capturing me, gripping me. The end was here. Sweating, I awoke from my slumber...

Adnaan Sheth (15)
Eden Boys' School Preston, Preston

Regret

Don't go in the woods, they told him. But, as a young child who loved to go on adventures, he ignored the person who told him to not go there. Within seconds of entering the creepy woods, he found himself in a trap. Desperately screaming for help and his parents, he was hanging upside down for over an hour. After his throat started to hurt and he couldn't scream anymore, the worst thing happened... footsteps. Large thuds banged against the soil and approached the innocent, vulnerable, young boy. The creature grabbed the boy and then he was never seen again...

Abdullah Azam Dadabhoy (15)

Eden Boys' School Preston, Preston

Death Taker

I looked around, desperately looking for an escape. They were after me because they were scared of what I could do. They thought I would use it for destruction. They didn't trust me, even after I had told them 1000 times I wouldn't use it to kill. However, I could use it to take death away. They didn't see the power I could use. *Oh no! They're here! They're close!* I could hear their footsteps, they were outside the door. They were going to break it down...
"Open up or we'll break it down."
They broke the door...

Muhammed Mualaz Patel (14)
Eden Boys' School Preston, Preston

A Warm Welcome

I knew there would be consequences, but I did it anyway. As I plunged into the gaping porthole, my mind began to compartmentalize the flashes of sheer happiness in my life. Was this the ending of a brief storm? I landed. I had company. Cherishing the fact that I had new chapters to write, I began to survey my pitch-black surroundings. Over-arching trees, out-of-place bushes, but pin-drop silence. The moon attempted to act as a flashlight, peeping through the tangles. Suddenly, I was gasping for air. Eyes wide open, my feet were dragged off. Was this the end?

Abdullah Desai (15)
Eden Boys' School Preston, Preston

Curiosity Killed The Cat

Don't go in the woods, they told me. Curiosity killed the cat. The cat that stood in front of me would probably kill me. It was more of a beast than a cat. A heart-rendering growl emitted from its snarling mouth. My heart momentarily left my body, desperate to escape from this hideous, vicious beast. Its beady eyes locked on me; I could almost feel them piercing through my petrified skull. A shiver snaked down my back, sweat beads pelted the ground. Its glistening, pitch-black body rippled with muscles. It snarled and leapt, no words escaped my mouth.

Ubaid Ibrahim (16)
Eden Boys' School Preston, Preston

A Psycho's Game

"You can only save one," the voice said.
My mother was tied down to the set of tracks on the left, my boyfriend tied to the tracks on the right. I was in a room, playing a psycho's game. Both my mother and boyfriend, with their heads raised, focused their eyes on me. With shame and guilt, I steered the lever left. A spiteful look from my mother's eyes stunned me as I looked down in shame. She sealed her eyes, accepting her fate. The train roared forwards, but it went right... What just happened? Would my mother forgive me?

Jaafer Kazi (15)
Eden Boys' School Preston, Preston

Missing

"Don't go in the woods," they told me.
But me and my brother had to get our missing friend out. We had both suffered through this dangerous journey and had fought beasts upon beasts. But the woods were just the beginning. We set off into the forest of death. We walked and walked, but then suddenly, something moved in front of us just a few metres away. We had to pretend that we didn't see it and walked on cautiously. I could feel its presence in front of me. My hand was ready and... *slash!* I had killed the beast.

Raihaan Suleman (15)
Eden Boys' School Preston, Preston

The Escape

She stepped in and questioned her choices with a worrying face.
He grabbed her head and smacked her against the cupboards. His superior ego boosted his rage. His crescent tattoo made him feel invincible as he had a gang. Choking on blood, she barely spoke but found the words to beg. He knew she was inferior so slapped her across her open wounds, spilling more blood, then stepped outside. She decided to run away, reaching a motorway. She got into a car coming her way. Her heart dropped as she saw the same crescent moon tattoo on his arm...

Jameel Mohammed (14)
Eden Boys' School Preston, Preston

Horror House

The child stepped into the gothic room. How did he get here? Before he could recall the events of the last hour, a creak in the floorboards sent a chill up his spine as his tender body started to shake. It started raining outside as the wind howled ferociously. A crash of lightning sent tears streaking down the child's cheeks. Suddenly, the lights flickered off. There was a crash, then a howl, followed by a gurgle and a final scream before a silence cloaked the house. Once again, the lights flickered back on to reveal an empty room...

Zayd Saeed (15)
Eden Boys' School Preston, Preston

Possessed: My Story

There he was, on the bed. I prayed it was a phase of being unconscious, yet there were no signs of life. The marks on his neck from the make-shift noose were prominent enough to be seen as self-inflicted. His eyes flickered as I began to move closer and opened subconsciously as I stood over him. He looked me in the eye and I saw a flash of anger moments before he lashed out at me and began screaming, "It's all your fault! I swear, it's all his fault!"
He backed off into the corner and slumped like a log.

Muaaz Kaba (15)
Eden Boys' School Preston, Preston

A Way Out

There was danger in there, they told me. The longing for the pure adrenaline had forced me through the woods. Slowly, I began to regret my decision as I got a strong smell of blood and rotting food. As the hours ticked by, my logic fell ever so slightly into an abyss of hopelessness and I began to grow weary and sore. A few miles later, I came across a small house built only out of wood, which surprisingly looked pretty sturdy. I approached with caution, only when I was close did I see the sign: *Enter If You Dare...*

Bilaal Patel (15)
Eden Boys' School Preston, Preston

The Escape

The door opened as a hairy, blood-thirsty beast ran after the innocent, English foreigner. He was frightened. What should he do? The car was three and a half miles away. His heart thumped, his pulse was rising, his body was shaking, he couldn't take anymore! He was going to fall on the ground and become dinner. His lungs were screaming from the need to run a little longer. Why was he so slow? He had been first in school marathons. His eyes were blurry, the beast was running faster. He couldn't outrun it...

Mohammed Awais Khan (14)
Eden Boys' School Preston, Preston

The Escape

I looked around, desperately searching for an escape. There was a fire in the building. Everyone started to scream as it was an emergency and ran out of the building. I was so sick of hearing people shouting and one of the guys called the firemen. I then realised that we were going to be rescued. Five minutes later, the firemen came as the fire started to get hotter. People were dying from the fire as I quickly ran as fast as I could to jump out of the building. I was so happy to see myself alive...

Umar Bhuta (15)
Eden Boys' School Preston, Preston

Mysterious Beast

In the forest, there was a wild animal. It was fierce and frightening to everyone and scary and everyone was afraid to go into the forest. It was a deep, dark place. The few people who had been brave enough to go in had never come back out. From stories of those who claimed to have come out alive, the beast was the size of a human adult. It had thick, white fur all over its body and dark, red eyes that stood out, fangs that came out with blood dripping. It was a four-legged beast. It was a wolf.

Mohammed Zaid Gurjee (15)
Eden Boys' School Preston, Preston

Mad Murder

Today, I hired someone to solve my murder but I did not know that he was the murderer of my beloved friend, Tom. The man who I hired, his name was John Wick. He lived in a town called Tilted Towers. He was very tall, always wore a black suit. My friend was a very nice person, lovely, caring and polite. I now started to realise that I had made a big mistake by hiring Mr John. He was acting very strangely and intimidatingly. He said that the killer was untraceable and was very sorry...

Abd-Us-Sami Khan (14)
Eden Boys' School Preston, Preston

Never Go To The Woods

My torch flickered and went out. Now I could no longer see the tall, shiny trees. I tried to find my way, but I saw some light guiding my way. They were wee, bright fireflies. I could hear aggressive, pushy rustles nearby and I saw no fireflies. I tried to see what had happened, but nothing was there. I tried to figure out what it was, but then I clearly saw a black figure spying on me behind the tree. I ran really fast. As soon as I looked over my shoulder, I saw it chasing me...

Anas Mahmood (11)
Eden Boys' School Preston, Preston

The Mysterious Thing

My torch flickered and went out. I couldn't see a thing, but I could hear... I could hear movement close by. I didn't know what it was. I moved my hand, trying to feel what was in front of me and around me, but I couldn't feel a thing. Just as I thought I couldn't feel anything, I felt it. It was slimy and much smaller than me. I had no idea what it was. I turned around and tried to get away from it but it kept following me. I turned around and it kidnapped me.

Shakeel Mohammed (15)
Eden Boys' School Preston, Preston

The Masked Figure

I looked around, desperately searching for an escape... The air got thinner and thinner. Gas filled the air. Sirens echoed throughout the house. Ashes shot out from the flames. Suddenly, a face shot through the corridor. Something grabbed my wrist. I turned around, nothing was there. I closed my eyes, hoping this was a dream, but it wasn't. The masked figure ran past the door whilst the flames spread through the house. I heard a voice from outside the door and then, that second, something pulled me across the room.
"There's only one escape!" exclaimed the mysterious, unknown voice...

Daisy Mai Thew (11)
Monkwearmouth Academy, Seaburn Dene

The Hostage

"You can only save one," he mumbled in a ramshackle, abandoned hut in the dense, dark forest.
The news bellowed on about the kidnapping. The phone rang, it was the detective trying to persuade the kidnapper to release the hostages. Men huddled around the door, guns pointed at everyone.
"Like I said, you can only save one!"
Suddenly, thuds started coming from the door. Everyone turned. It smashed open, police screamed and pointed guns at everyone. Two days later, everything was normal, life was fine. The kidnapper had been locked up in prison, but it would happen again...

Archie Cattanach (11)
Monkwearmouth Academy, Seaburn Dene

Horror House

I looked around, desperately searching for an escape...
Smash!
"Where are you, little midget?!"
My heart was pounding. The only reason I was in this house was because my stupid friend threw a ball through the window. I held my breath. I could smell the monster's stench coming closer. Slowly, I could feel cold sweat running down my forehead.
"I'm coming for you. I can sense that I'm getting closer and closer..."
As silent and as quickly as I could, I made my way to a different room. I was too late, the monster pounced. My heart stopped...

Lucy-Alice Flatley (11)
Monkwearmouth Academy, Seaburn Dene

Trapped

I looked around, desperately searching for an escape. I could hear voices outside.
"Help!" I screamed.
My voice echoed off the metal walls. It was no use, my heart beat faster and faster. I heard a car pull up outside. The door opened and slammed. I pressed my ear against the cold wall.
"It's ready," a deep voice groaned.
There were some stomach-churning creaks, then silence. The crate began to rock from side to side. I lost my balance and fell to the ground. I could hear shouting. *Bang!* Just then, sunlight flooded into the crate. I was saved!

Amelia Bennett (11)
Monkwearmouth Academy, Seaburn Dene

Jordan's Heroics

"You can save only one," the voice bellowed.
Jordan Pickdord was the name. It was time for Jordan. He'd succumbed to a lot of unfair, undeserved criticism over recent days. With deep, concentrated breathing, he focussed on the enormous challenge he had come face-to-face with. The honour, the pride that would come within the next four milli-seconds, it was tangible, it was almost worthy of touching. Jordan stood, tall like the Empire State Building, jumped, sending seismic waves across the view. The sweat dripped down his face one by one. He stepped up and saved the pennants.

Nathan Spence (15)
Monkwearmouth Academy, Seaburn Dene

Am I Really Dead?

"Wake me up, please!"
The words made my brain boil. I had recently started a murder investigation, but I hadn't been told the victim's name. Until now. My boss shoved a pile of sheets onto my unorganised desk. Without looking up from my computer, I said, "When do you want it done by?"
"Friday, if you can."
I muttered an 'okay' as I typed. Exhausted, I took a long sip of my lukewarm latte, glancing around my office. My hazel eyes scanned the papers. Then, I saw the name. My name. My face. My brain boiled. Was I really dead?

Eve Rodgers (11)
Monkwearmouth Academy, Seaburn Dene

Don't Go In The Woods

Don't go in the woods, they told me as they'd heard some news about some eerie activity happening in there. 'Keep out', 'danger', 'stay away', that was all I could hear.
12.30 at night, the door creaked open as my foot slipped out. A breeze blasted towards my face and then I slipped into the darkness. I shut the door slowly and carefully, trying not to make a noise, and then trotted away past the fence, past the warning signs and into the woods. Lots of sounds were heard, but I suddenly heard a loud one in the distance... *Crack!*

Sidney Young (11)
Monkwearmouth Academy, Seaburn Dene

All Was Well...

The torch flickered and went out. Newt had found himself in the middle of the woods. His friend had disappeared. The result of this led to Newt looking for his dearest friend, Minho. In the blink of an eye, he was teleported. Minho was lying there, motionless, breathless.
"Oh no!" shouted Newt.
He couldn't believe his eyes. Tears started falling, their sweetest memories started to fly back into his head. Then he was interrupted. A large, fierce animal stepped out of the darkness. It pounced at Newt. He could feel its teeth digging into his skin...

Kuba Baczkiewicz (11)
Monkwearmouth Academy, Seaburn Dene

The Figure In The Dark

Don't go into the woods, my parents told me before I left.
After a while, I approached the woods.
"Don't go into the woods," I repeated again.
I turned my back, the dark of the forest called my name. I stepped into the woods. The further I walked, the more nervous I became. It felt like a million eyes were watching me. Movement caught my attention. I wasn't alone. I had to run. I struggled to breathe, the woods seemed never-ending. The figure was gone. When I stopped running, I found he wasn't gone, he was standing over me...

Lily Cowperthwaite (11)
Monkwearmouth Academy, Seaburn Dene

The Scream Before The Silence

Don't go in the woods, they told me. How I wish I'd listened. As my torch shone on the twisting trees, I thought I was alone. The twigs beneath my feet started to snap, each one sending chills down my spine. Then I heard it. The scream. It was just as they'd said. The horrifying sound echoed throughout the woods before silence fell. I was stunned, fear glueing me to the spot. Leaves started to rustle around me without any wind moving them. As my torch scanned the terrifying woods, looking for something or someone, I realised I wasn't alone...

Jasmine Graydon (14)
Monkwearmouth Academy, Seaburn Dene

The Beast

As I walked towards the woods, I saw a hooded figure and they said, "Don't go in the woods."
I then placed my ear against the branches and I heard a roar. I peered through the branches and saw a creature. It had glowing, amber eyes and muddy, brown hair spread across its body. It then bared its sharp teeth, showing black saliva. The hooded figure appeared again.
"Don't blink in its sight or you'll never see the light of day."
A sudden urge took over me as I needed to blink. I wanted to blink, I blinked...

Sophie Hale (11)
Monkwearmouth Academy, Seaburn Dene

The Package

"Tell me everything you know, child," were the words my abductor said to me as the potato bag got peeled off my face.

The dimly-lit room was unknown to me as well as the two men who were standing in front of me, holding a parcel in their grubby hands. It was the packages of something I was given to deliver from my uncle.

"Where were you taking these drugs then, son?" they viciously demanded.

I thought this must have been a joke, so a reply wasn't given. It wasn't until I heard the shotgun that I realised...

Oliver Goshorn (15)

Monkwearmouth Academy, Seaburn Dene

Encounter

The dilophosaurus ran through the dense forest, not looking back, terrified of what was following him. The dilophosaurus had no chance of outpacing his predators. He then ran to a tree, hoping for the chance he could climb it. He wasn't so lucky as a pack of velociraptors surrounded him. Their jaws were filled with blood and their teeth were red. The dilophosaurus was shaking as the raptors came closer and closer to him. The dilophosaurus started to cry until he saw something in the sky. The raptors noticed it and then ran off. It was the end...

Aaron Alan Lang (13)
Monkwearmouth Academy, Seaburn Dene

Serial Killer

I never thought I'd have to do this: solve the murder of my own brother. He was just standing there, waiting. We'd found the murder weapon; a Nike shoe. We stayed up all night, but we had finally solved the mystery. We watched the CCTV and uncovered it. It was Billy Berry... he threw my brother on the floor. What a height from the tallest shelf! He jumped onto his chest until he broke his box. Why would someone kill a box of Rice Krispies cereal?
"Sleep with one eye open Billy, we are coming for you... we are coming..."

Maizie Lily Berry (11)
Monkwearmouth Academy, Seaburn Dene

Captive

I looked around, desperately searching for an escape. Only days before, I was free, but now I was captive with five minutes of light and ten minutes of air. My eyes darted around, scanning the room for a crack in the wall, a drop of water in the corner... Nothing. My life was as frail as a feather, as hopeless as a newborn's. Blackness consumed the room. I curled up in the corner, unaware of the timer beeping in the distance. Slipping away from life itself, my head was filled with the screaming of the people I'd previously murdered.

Beth Hutchinson (11)
Monkwearmouth Academy, Seaburn Dene

Don't Go In The Woods

Don't go in the woods, they told me. Turn back for your own good, they begged. Fools. They were too scared from stories passed down from their parents and their parents before them. They were simpletons, believing in Pagan superstition. This beast would be nothing more than an angered bear or at worst, a cross-breed between a wolf and a bear. Strange, there were no birds or anything, just trees. I'd been walking for hours and nothing. I wanted my reward for killing the animal...
"What is that?"
God help me...

Niall Armstrong (16)
Monkwearmouth Academy, Seaburn Dene

Decisions

Please let this be a dream, I thought. I screamed at the top of my lungs, "I love you, Jacob!"
"I love-"
The floor dropped from underneath him. The crowd went silent, the only sound that could be heard was the creaking of the rope which Jacob hung from. I let out a deafening cry as I slumped to my knees in agony, breaking the silence which rang through the auditorium. The love of my life was gone and it was my fault. It was his life or our child's and I chose the child. Jacob was gone forever.

Lauren Hutchinson (15)
Monkwearmouth Academy, Seaburn Dene

Consequences

I knew there would be consequences, but I did it anyway. I tiptoed downstairs and into the kitchen. I grabbed the keys to the door. After I'd unlocked the door, I ran out into the front garden. I circled the house, but nothing was in sight. What was that noise? I gave up and went back inside. I lay in bed, then I heard another noise. This time it was in my bedroom. I saw a shadow, it lingered over me... He pulled something from his pocket. The shadow looked familiar. I remembered my mother's murder...
"Help me!"

Caitlin Eve Gibbins (11)
Monkwearmouth Academy, Seaburn Dene

The Escape

"You can save only one," the voice mumbled on this day in October.
There was a murderer next to my house. On that day, my next-door neighbour rang me and said, "Your wife's dead."
I burst into tears, my life was over. All of a sudden... *Bang!* I was in a bunker with two people holding guns at me and shouting, "Tell me everything!"
I started shouting and screaming, but no one could hear me. I was too far away from everyone. I was dead. I got out. I ran at them... *Bang!*

Ben Charlton (11)
Monkwearmouth Academy, Seaburn Dene

The Dark Ending

My torch flickered and went out. It felt like I had been blinded, it was so dark. I wished my torch hadn't gone out so I could see again. My heart pounded and I couldn't breathe. I heard whispering in the distance. It was a horrible creature. My heart stopped, I looked around desperately for an escape. I pulled the covers over my head and my mischievous cat shot out of the door. Finally, I'd escaped this terrible nightmare. I heard a sigh of relief and settled back down. Suddenly, I heard a scream from downstairs...

Elliot Stephenson (11)
Monkwearmouth Academy, Seaburn Dene

The Figure Behind The Tree

Don't go in the woods, they told me. I should've listened. As I walked through the endless stretch of trees illuminated only by my torch, I suddenly heard a leaf crunch to my left. I stopped in my tracks and listened, all I could hear now was the rapid thud of my heart pounding against my chest. The snap of a branch snapping behind me made me hastily turn around. I saw the silhouette of a person quickly step behind a tree. That was it! I started sprinting in the opposite direction. Then as I tripped, I saw the figure...

Daniel Merrington (14)
Monkwearmouth Academy, Seaburn Dene

The Dark Forest

Don't go in the woods, they told me, but I did it anyway. I went in very slowly, nothing happened. There was a man in black, he was seven metres away. He was talking in a very quiet voice, "You should not be here, why did you trespass on my land?"
I couldn't see the man's face, it was covered by his hoodie. He slowly walked towards me, he had a crowbar in his hands. He said, "You can't get out of this area."
I ran away to my house and promised myself to not go in the woods again...

Sulaiman Al Sulaimani (12)

Monkwearmouth Academy, Seaburn Dene

The Nightmare

Please let this be a dream, I thought as I drifted off to sleep. As I drifted off to sleep, a figure popped into my head. It was a dark figure which didn't show its face. It was a bad figure that haunted everyone. It was like someone crawling into your body and haunting you. The dream always started as the black figure came towards you. The figure flickered back with lights flickering off and on. People around you in the outside world would only see you in a deep sleep, but they never knew what went on inside...

Antonia Elliott (13)
Monkwearmouth Academy, Seaburn Dene

The Break-In

Suddenly, the time came to commit the crime. My heart was beating faster than ever as I entered the house through the smashed window behind me. I wasn't thinking when I entered. Screaming in shock, the owners were home. I looked around, desperately searching for an escape. I couldn't let them catch me. Fortunately, there was an exit right in front of me. I sprinted for my life as I heard a voice, "Stop! I'm from the police force!"
I had been caught and I regretted everything I had done that day...

Maimi Holyoak-Goss (11)
Monkwearmouth Academy, Seaburn Dene

Why Didn't I Listen?

Don't go in the woods, they told me, but I didn't listen. The forest was dark, misty and mysterious; there had been reports of missing people and I was one of them. That horrible, heart-breaking day was still with me. All I remembered was me looking around for my younger brother who had run away from home. But as I slowly leaned into the dead, small bush... I fell. It was like someone had pushed me. I saw my brother and men and women who had disappeared, chanting, "We told you not to go in the forest!"

Hayley Bell (11)
Monkwearmouth Academy, Seaburn Dene

The Haunted Mansion

I looked around, desperately searching for an escape. I wanted to get out as soon as possible. With heart pounding and ideas filling up my mind, I quickly searched for an escape plan. I couldn't bear looking back. Suddenly, I heard an ear-piercing noise come from upstairs in the haunted mansion. Then I heard a door creaking and loud thumps on the stairs. All the doors were locked. Did I dare look and see what was there? Wishing I was home and trying not to make any noise, I slowly started to peer over my shoulder...

Lola Collier (11)
Monkwearmouth Academy, Seaburn Dene

The Final Run

I knew there would be consequences, but I did it anyway. It was late one Friday night, we had made our last deal. We were taking our secret shortcut through the woods. The time was 1am. About five minutes into the woods, a sharp, deceiving rattling trailed behind us and, without thinking, we shot in any direction we could. We couldn't afford to lose our supply. Distant screams and shouts were heard. I didn't think about stopping. I could see the light in the distance. I was almost out when someone aimed at me...

Josh Hewitt (15)
Monkwearmouth Academy, Seaburn Dene

In The Woods

Don't go in the woods, they told me, however, I was suspicious so I went in. The woods were gloomy and pitch-black. All of a sudden, I heard strange noises and the noises were getting louder and louder. They sounded like animal noises. I started to get scared. The want to run was starting to get the better of me. Suddenly, the noises grew louder and louder. I started to make an escape. I ran for my life. Instantly, the strange, loud screams and noises stopped. I looked around desperately to see what had happened...

Jaxon Telford (11)
Monkwearmouth Academy, Seaburn Dene

Haunted Woods

Please let this be a dream, I thought to myself. I was running through the woods whilst my mum was being attacked by these zombie-looking creatures. They told us not to go into the woods, but we didn't listen. We should've! I was petrified, exhausted. I was shaking. Was I going to live? Or would this be the end? The wind was howling like a distressed dog. The night sky was black and red, like it was staring into my soul. I tripped over a log, they were right behind me! What was going to happen to me?

Morgan Regan (13)
Monkwearmouth Academy, Seaburn Dene

No Souls Left

"You can save only one," the voice said as my parents were hanging in cages.
I was mortified as I could only choose one to live. My mother was crying, so I said, "I don't want to choose."
So the voice said, "You could save both if you sacrifice yourself."
It was a painful decision, but I decided that saving two lives was better than one. I sacrificed myself. There was a loud gunshot that echoed loudly around the room. That led me here on the anniversary of my death...

Kate Kirkwood (14)
Monkwearmouth Academy, Seaburn Dene

Paranoid Party

Please let this be a dream, I thought as I clenched my fist in alarm. I jumped with fear.
"Phew," I sighed.
I talked to my parents, asking for a party. Finally, they said yes. I planned it but had this dream about the party. I was doing something with my friends, shrieks burst out my mouth, but that didn't stop me... That night was very long and painful. I lay in bed, sat on the bar, getting scars, cried my eyes out, called my mam, lay in a hospital bed... Never again, never again!

Brooke Veitch (11)
Monkwearmouth Academy, Seaburn Dene

The End

Please let this be a dream, I thought. We were all handed a piece of paper stating what our future would hold. Mine was blank. As the thunder and lightning roared, the telephone buzzed.

"This is the end," it said in a dramatic voice.

I placed the phone back on the rack. What did this mean? Who was that? A million questions filled my wandering mind. How was I going to die today? A very loud bang filled my ears and I could feel my mind leave my body. I realised, this really was my end...

Stephanie Peebles (11)
Monkwearmouth Academy, Seaburn Dene

Held Hostage

"You can only save one, Toby," whispered my mother.

The sight I was looking at was so depressing. My dad's bank was being held hostage. Ten people. My mouth made the shape of an 'o' as I stood still, gazing. I didn't want anyone to die. I ran, confused. A gun was pointing at them. I jumped and kicked the gun out of his hand. I hesitated, grabbed my dad and we ran to the exit. Luckily, I had the gun. I broke it. I ran back and the building crashed down. I sat and cried my eyes out...

Nathan Doyle (11)
Monkwearmouth Academy, Seaburn Dene

Same Fate

"Goodnight! And remember, don't come out of your room."
I heard my mother's command and tried to obey. I crawled up the stairs, trying not to wake my sister. *Slam!* The door to the cupboard shut. What was my mother doing?
'Dear Diary,
My mum has told me not to come out of my room, I just hope that she will not do the same thing to my sister as she did to my dad...'
I heard a noise. I peeped out of the crack in my door... My mum was hanging from the ceiling...

Daniel Green (11)
Monkwearmouth Academy, Seaburn Dene

Chased

Don't go in the woods, they told me. But of course I did and what a mistake that was. My flashlight had just died. I thought I was being followed. There was something in the bushes, I could hear it breaking branches. It was running at me. It was chasing me, I could hear it. My flashlight was working again, barely. I didn't think it would work for long. I saw someone. I thought I was saved. Something was wrong, the person didn't look human. I couldn't see the thing that was chasing me... Unless...

Charley Nicholas (11)
Monkwearmouth Academy, Seaburn Dene

The Torch That Went Out

As me and my friend started walking into the forest, we only had a torch. We walked further and further into the forest until the torch started acting up. It was turning off and turning on. It was starting to creep us out. We kept walking until the torch stopped working. My friend screamed and then he disappeared. *Please let this be a dream,* I thought to myself. I started shivering and shaking. I thought I should go home so I started running towards my house. I never looked back to the woods ever again.

Keane Thompson (12)
Monkwearmouth Academy, Seaburn Dene

The Escape

I knew there would be consequences, but I did it anyway. My parents would be ashamed of me, but I had to do it. I crept to the woods, stopped, then walked straight in. As soon as I was in, something felt wrong. I wasn't sure what it was. It was like someone was following me. I turned, it turned. I carried on walking... *Crack!* I turned like lightning. Behind me stood a man, an evil smile cracked on his face. He carried a knife with blood on it. I began to shiver.
"Run!" I told myself.

Eve Errington (11)
Monkwearmouth Academy, Seaburn Dene

Mask Massacre

Don't go in the woods, they said. I was too stupid to listen and I still went in. Walking around, I suddenly realised I was lost. Walking all directions, there was no sign of getting out. I started to panic and I ran. Suddenly, I slipped down a bank into a river and I hit my head. I screamed for help and a voice spoke. It said, "You're mine."
A masked man, cut and bleeding, appeared. He jumped down the bank with his machete and swung it at me. I dodged it. He swung it again. It hit me...

Kaden Ellis (12)
Monkwearmouth Academy, Seaburn Dene

What's In There?

Don't go in the woods, they told me. Strange things had been happening. In past weeks, many had gone in those mysterious woods, but none had returned. I thought I'd be the first, I was going to, I would return. I entered, hoping to return. It was dull and silent as I trekked further and further into the woods. There was a slight rustle in the bushes. My hairs stood up like a ghost had passed my arm. Terrified, I hastily scanned around. Then I saw it, that thing. I then realised I wouldn't return...

Nathan McAdam (15)
Monkwearmouth Academy, Seaburn Dene

Mamma's Coming!

My torch flickered and went out. I started to scream in my head. Quickly, I looked all around me to find her... There, right there. I saw two red eyes in the corner and she spoke to me, "Mamma will look after you."
In my head, I said, *that's what happens when you open your presents early*. I started running but tried not to make a noise because she always knew where I was. I got to the basement and locked it, holding my breath. I could hear her calling for me. I just stayed still...

Annalise B Bawn (14)
Monkwearmouth Academy, Seaburn Dene

Horror Of My Life

I looked around, desperately searching for a way out. The minute I took a step into the forest, some sort of giant wall came up and blocked my only way out. Loads of different paths appeared, five different ones. The first one had lightning and all the others were just plain. I went with my lucky number, path number three but, when I went down the path, I saw werewolves. Then a half-man, half-horse (a centaur) appeared. They both came after me. I managed to dodge them, but some sort of zombie army appeared...

Callum Coates (12)
Monkwearmouth Academy, Seaburn Dene

The Shed

I looked around, desperately searching for an escape. It was dark in there and a sudden clap of thunder overhead startled me as I backed up against the wooden door. The windows shook as the wind forced them to cave in. The glass smashed onto the cement ground, leaving thousands of tiny segments all over. My face was now bleeding. My hands were sweating. I heard the back door slam shut. Seconds later, a figure raced out into the back garden and leapt over the fence. He or she had their pockets full of cash...

Megan Gorgulu (11)
Monkwearmouth Academy, Seaburn Dene

The Escape

I looked around, desperately searching for an escape. I tried to get free from the rope tying my hands but I couldn't. There were loads of people walking around the buildings. One of them came in and said, "Stand up!"
So I did. He took me to the boat that they brought me on. There were loads of people on there who were sitting there scared. I never said a word, I just sat there, worrying where I was and where they were taking me. I saw land and I ran away from them. I was free at last.

Molly Ann Brown (12)
Monkwearmouth Academy, Seaburn Dene

Terrible Attack Starts!

Don't go in the woods, they told me, but I did. It was dark and spooky, all you could hear was birds whistling. Leaves crunched as I walked. Suddenly, it rained. I didn't want to leave, but it was getting scary. I could hear someone, but I didn't act scared. I must have fallen asleep because I woke up with my hair all messy. I got up and started walking again. Someone was shouting. Out the corner of my eye, someone was trying to kill this man. He had him against the tree and had a knife.

Kiera Jo Armstrong (12)
Monkwearmouth Academy, Seaburn Dene

The Girl Who Came Back

My torch flickered and went out, then a light appeared against the wall. What was it? It hovered against me and disappeared. It came back again. It looked like a little girl, but then I realised it was starting to talk. It said, "I love you to the moon and back."
That was weird, my mam said that to me. She was at the shop, buying my tea. I focused on the ghost. The police rang... They said that my mam had died half an hour ago when I first came up to my room... The ghost was my mam.

Martin Robert Skinner (11)
Monkwearmouth Academy, Seaburn Dene

Lost In The Woods

Don't Enter, the sign said... but I was wondering what was in there. I went in, I entered the woods. At first, it was fine but I started to hear suspicious noises. They were getting closer to my ears. All of a sudden, I heard a loud scream close to me, as if someone was getting hurt, so I ran to the scream. It was only a bat, but the noises were getting closer and closer so I decided to run. As the noises got closer, I found a way out. *Please let this be a dream*, I thought...

Ted Norman Knaggs (11)
Monkwearmouth Academy, Seaburn Dene

The Haunted Woods

A long time ago, five girls had a sleepover. They put the radio on and heard something about a haunted wood not far from them. They wanted to go to see if the wood was actually haunted.
When the girls got there, they saw a strange, creepy guy. They thought he was trying to hide, if he was, he wasn't very good. Suddenly, the guy started to follow them. Ally told them all to split up. They did, but the guy followed the three girls. Near them was a fence. Only three of them climbed over...

Lily Kempster (11)
Monkwearmouth Academy, Seaburn Dene

The Great Escape

I looked around, desperately searching for an escape. I tried and tried, but there was no escape. I didn't even know where I was or what happened to me. I thought I'd been kidnapped. Who'd taken me? I kept asking myself all of these questions over and over again.
Finally, someone came into the room. I thought they were going to rescue me, but it didn't look like it. I told him to come into the light and show himself and when he did I was so afraid. He was a monster! Help!

Lucy Green (12)
Monkwearmouth Academy, Seaburn Dene

Secrets

The alley was dark and sinister, it smelled like fish, but I saw smoke coming out of the alley. I was suspicious so I walked in daringly.

"Tell me everything you know, child," a man said.

I ran because I wasn't going to tell the man I hadn't even seen him, but slowly, my skin turned pale, my veins were showing. I felt dead. I couldn't breathe and I died. How could I tell this story? I was haunting the world around me as a ghost. I would kill anyone I saw...

Lewis Nelson (11)
Monkwearmouth Academy, Seaburn Dene

Escape

It was in the middle of the night and we were out in the woods.
"Don't go in the woods," they'd warned us before, but it was too late.
We knew there would be consequences, but we did it anyway. Now we were lost. We tried to call home but we couldn't get a signal. We didn't know what to do.
Wandering through the woods, we desperately searched for a way out, but it was hopeless. We aimlessly walked through the woods, then I saw it: an escape.

Caitlin Brown (11)
Monkwearmouth Academy, Seaburn Dene

The Death!

Don't go in the woods, they told me. I went in. I was in there for thirty minutes before my torch went out. I could see nothing but darkness. The only thing I remembered was that my friends told me not to go in when I woke up. I'd been in hospital with police surrounding me. They were asking what I remembered. I said nothing. They called for the nurse, they took her outside. She came in and asked for the clothes I was wearing that night so they could do some tests.

Aaleayah Cross (13)
Monkwearmouth Academy, Seaburn Dene

The Mysterious Woods!

I desperately persuaded myself not to enter the woods as they had told me. A big, hairy creature was hidden deep in the woods, beneath a den. Edging my way forwards, and with a nervous look on my face, I was determined to find this weird creature. Getting closer and closer to the place where they'd told me it wandered, a quick shiver tickled my spine and there appeared huge, yellow eyes. They followed me everywhere and then I reminded myself of all the consequences...

Kaitlyn Fairbridge (11)
Monkwearmouth Academy, Seaburn Dene

Clinton Road

I looked around, desperately searching for an escape to leave the house. There was a loud bang from the corridor. There was someone chasing me outside the house. He chased me down Clinton Road. There were so many trucks going past me. Clinton Road had many bent trees hanging over it. I found a car in the middle of the road and I got into it. There was a bloke in the back seat. I didn't think of it...
I went back to the house and it was all a dream.

Reece Shields (12)
Monkwearmouth Academy, Seaburn Dene

The Woods

Don't go in the woods, they said. Now look at me, dead. I was driving down a long, winding road in the dark. I stopped at the side of the road to get some rest but, all of a sudden, as soon as I got settled, I heard scratching down the side of my car. And there I was, stood face-to-face with a bright yellow, beady figure. Back home, my friends had warned me not to go near the woods and I was in shock. I ran into the woods and that was the end of me...

Lauren Atkinson (13)
Monkwearmouth Academy, Seaburn Dene

The Unsolved Murder

Don't go in the woods, they told me and now I saw why. The police barricaded off the woods, but me and my friends found a way in. We went in but, little did I know, he was watching... He picked us off one by one until there was only one of us. I was the last one. I ran, but he was faster than me. He caught up and my life was gone. The police still had not caught him but I saw his every move. He lay and waited for prey. Now I watched him from above...

Daniel Richardson (11)
Monkwearmouth Academy, Seaburn Dene

The Night I Died!

My torch flickered and went out. I was all alone in the dark, walking along the roadside. I saw a light, it was an old street light that was flickering. Then I heard a scream and then a bang. I ran back, I was scared. Then I heard a gunshot. I didn't stop running. It was 10.55pm, I was meant to be home by 11pm, I was nowhere near home. My mam was going to kill me. I thought, *what am I going to do?* I didn't know what to do...

Millie Whitfield (13)
Monkwearmouth Academy, Seaburn Dene

Fright Night

I opened my eyes and I was tied up to a tree in the woods. I saw a small glimpse of light coming from a little cottage. I had to escape, I was starving. I could smell delicious waffles cooking on the grill. Out of the corner of my eye, I saw a thin twig so I grabbed it once I got the ties off. I ripped off the tape on my mouth and ran towards the cottage. There was a family sitting on a couch. I silently opened the door...
Bang!

Ruby Tough (12)
Monkwearmouth Academy, Seaburn Dene

Was It A Dream?

Bang! A door slammed shut. Pain rippled through my body. A knife was wedged into my left ankle and a bullet had pierced its way into my right hand. I wondered if this was a dream. For a good few moments, I heard an ambulance coming my way. The glass shattered and so did most of the bones in my arms and legs. The ambulance ran over me like I wasn't even there...

Lily Grace Dodd (11)
Monkwearmouth Academy, Seaburn Dene

Orders

My torch flickered and went out. I couldn't see anything. It was pitch-black. How did I end up here? I walked around. Suddenly, I felt a cramp. Then I fell to the ground. When I woke up, it was morning. I tried to get up but my arm was aching.
"Help! Help!" I screamed.
It was hopeless. No one was going to help me. I turned over and a tall man was stood there.
"I am here, do exactly as I say, or you will never escape."
"No!" I told him. "I won't listen to you!"
"Okay, well then..."

Leah Sanderson (13)
Richard Rose Morton Academy, Carlisle

The Railway

I knew there would be consequences, but I did it anyway. I had not listened to my parents by going to the old, rusty railway. Crashes and bangs filled the air. Shaking like a leaf, I ran to a bush, ducking under leaves, thinking to myself, *what's going on?* Hours passed by. Now running late, I stood up and looked around to see something moving in the distance. I started to run. I heard a loud scream, but then it had gone. My heart beat like a drum... *Boom!* Walking home, I sat and wondered what would happen next...

Lauren Paige Dowson (14)

Richard Rose Morton Academy, Carlisle

Catacombs

My torch flickered and went out. The silence and sudden darkness hit me like a truck. I was already missing the sound of the flames. Thinking about it, the torch sounded like a thundering boulder. I put my hands out and searched for the cold, damp walls. I then felt it. A dry bone. I continued walking, only to have more bones fall on me. Jangling bones clattered onto me. I was scared. It felt as if I was being attacked by an army of skeletons.
The catacombs are hell. I am stuck down here. I've been stuck for days...

Finlay Paul Pieri (13)
Richard Rose Morton Academy, Carlisle

I Thought It Was A Dream

Please let this be a dream... I didn't know where I was, all I remembered was going to sleep and I woke up not knowing where I was. I went to check the door and it was locked. My door didn't even have a lock! I heard a high-pitched sound in my right ear. I turned around and saw a bright light. I must've been dreaming, I had to be. I stepped forwards, I stepped and it pulled me towards it. I didn't want to go anywhere. I didn't know what to do. *Please, help me...* What could I do?

Ellie Bradley (13)
Richard Rose Morton Academy, Carlisle

Was I Dreaming?

Please let this be a dream, I thought to myself as I crept along the forest floor, my heart pounding deep in my chest, my breathing heavy. This was the fabled Lumwick Wood, no one had come out alive. A chill ran down my spine as I walked further down the path. Suddenly, I felt someone pull me into the bushes and hold a knife to my throat. Before I could scream, their clammy hand covered my mouth. I woke up instantly in a cold sweat, breathing deeply, my head searching around my room for danger...

Lauren Grantham (13)
Richard Rose Morton Academy, Carlisle

Down The Ravine

My torch flickered, it ran out. I was left alone, my only company was darkness. There was no way I could get back to the top of the ravine, even with my magic. Next thing I knew, I couldn't move. Then I saw the red eyes of a paralysaur; it was paralysing me, making me ready to eat. With the strength I had, I conjured a small ball using my magic, just enough to blow the beast back. I then killed it using a strong bolt of lightning. I should have used a taming spell; I would've had a friend...

Kieran Martin (13)
Richard Rose Morton Academy, Carlisle

The Adventure

My torch flickered and went out. I felt a cold breeze fly past me. I looked around to see what I could see and I made eye contact with a red-eyed beast. Its claws were sharp enough to pierce my skin, its wings were bigger than a great oak tree and strong enough to knock over buildings. Its teeth were sharp enough to snap your bones in half. It roared and fled to the sky, knocking me and some trees over. To this day, I had never seen anything like it, so I documented it in a study journal...

Tyler Dale Holmes (13)
Richard Rose Morton Academy, Carlisle

Don't Go In The Woods

Don't go in the woods, they told me, but I couldn't help it. The tension was building up, so I went in. I had to. I took my torch in with me. It was dark and gloomy and, even with my torch in my hands, I could hardly see anything. I stumbled through the old forest and I heard a noise. I was really scared and I didn't know what to do. I carried on walking. All of a sudden, there was a snap. I ran. I was so scared. Something touched me. My torch flickered and went out...

Alia Riley (13)
Richard Rose Morton Academy, Carlisle

Behind You

My torch flickered and went out, then something ran past me as quick as a jet. Then my torch went out and it felt like it was all eyes on me. Then there was a noise behind me. I tried to turn my torch back on, but the light wouldn't shine. The noise behind me got louder and louder, to the point that it was right behind me. I wanted to look, but I was scared to. I tried to knock my torch back on, then it flickered back on but there wasn't anyone in front of me...

Jemma Marie Rowe (14)
Richard Rose Morton Academy, Carlisle

The Sheep's Revenge

Please let this be a dream, I thought. As I left my room, I saw him lying down and, luckily, they got rid of the evidence. At least I felt fine. While I lay, I saw the sheep. This was bad. I woke up again and went. I went to my sister in shock, pure shock of how I had killed someone. I went to hide in case they found me. Hopefully, they wouldn't find me. I went to the woods with no torch, no help, just in case they tried to catch me...

Sean Edgar (13)
Richard Rose Morton Academy, Carlisle

A Quiet Night In... Restraints

"Tell me everything you know, child," he barked, his silhouette pacing back in front of me.
I couldn't see much through the bag on my head, but I knew to keep my breathing steady, panicking wouldn't help whatsoever. The bitter air filled my lungs and the deadly silence was broken with a conversation between two men.
"I don't think he's the one."
"He isn't," the other interrupted. "He doesn't know anything."
"We'll have to dispose of him then."
I began listening, the click of a gun... It was time to act.
"I can tell you, I know how she died!"

Harry Stead (14)
The Heath School, Runcorn

Don't Wander Into The Woods!

"Mum always tells me not to go into the woods, but for once, I want to see what is in there!"
Leon, the small, posh boy, wandered into the woods.
Everything changed from that day onwards.
"Hello!" he said as he didn't know there were monsters lurking behind him.
"Argh!"
The little boy, Leon, was gone, never to be seen again...
"Where is he? How has he disappeared?" his mum asked when the police said he'd gone missing and not been found.
His mother and father were scared by this terrifying experience of their little boy, Leon. He was gone.

Liam Hall (12)
The Heath School, Runcorn

Strangers

"Don't go in the woods," they told me as I was running towards it.
I shouted to them, "Why not?"
There was no reply. I repeated myself, not knowing there was something in the bushes. I said, "Why are you ignoring me?"
Again, no reply. Had time paused? Something was in the bushes. A voice came from the woods, "Psst!"
I saw a man with sweets in the bush.
"Come with me," he whispered.
I said, "Go away."
He started to come out of the bushes slowly and creepily. I froze. I didn't know what to do: run or stay...

Reuben Power (12)
The Heath School, Runcorn

The Cabin In The Woods

Don't go in the woods, they told me. I thought it'd be fun, ambitious, a new type of experience, a risk - aren't Sagittarius' risk takers? We came across something... a cabin.

"Stay overnight, it'll be fun!" they pressured.

Knock, knock, knock. The mossy, worn-out door creaked into the abyss of the abode. Floorboards cried for strength as we shuffled over them one by one. I was alarmed, uneasy for any scenario that was possible. Suddenly, a cacophony of echoes filled the room. Why was I doing this? What would the consequences be? Would I live to see tomorrow?

Natalie Nosal (14)
The Heath School, Runcorn

Searching For Hope

I looked around, desperately searching for an escape, turning each corner, hoping for freedom and relief from this torturous agony I had been made to endure. Would I get out alive? This was my responsibility and I had blown it, regretting every moment since the very beginning. I thought I was just over exaggerating, I always over exaggerated. Suddenly, light struck me but it wasn't the way out, someone was coming towards me slowly. I wasn't alone. The light was blinding me. I couldn't see how it was all in my head, going around. Finally, I found the way out...

Kia Keats (12)
The Heath School, Runcorn

Be Aware Of Your Surroundings

Don't venture in the woods, he told me. I didn't listen, but he replied, "I warned you."
He disappeared into the darkness. He scared me, but I carried on anyway. Suddenly, I saw a figure. *I should have listened,* I thought, but I was drawn to see what it was. It darted behind a tree as fast as I could blink. I tried to run, but then, there it was: its black, sharp claws, its orange eyes... It reached out for me. My feet were stuck. I couldn't do anything. It whispered, "You should have listened."
I was definitely dead...

Tom Spencer (12)
The Heath School, Runcorn

Cabin

"Don't go in the woods," they told me as I stared into the dark woods.
I kept hearing voices saying, "Come in, don't be scared."
I couldn't stop myself. I walked into the woods and saw a cabin.
"Come in," a man said, staring at me.
I walked backwards, then I fell over on a slippery branch. I felt really sleepy, all I saw next was horrifying. He was changing into an animal! He dragged me into the cabin. There were animals hanging everywhere. I felt a hammer hit my head, then it was dark. Death was near...

Anthony Davis (12)
The Heath School, Runcorn

Hopeless And Helpless

I looked around, desperately searching for an escape as I panicked uncontrollably. Suddenly, an ominous lit lamp sparked to life, beneath it was a rusty, old lock. I crawled over to it, completely exhausted from panicking. The lamp had a piece of frayed string glued to it. The string held a rusty key and a crusty note. Carefully, I removed the note and fumbled with it whilst trying to open it with my weak fingers. After a while, I managed to unfurl it from its crumpled state.
Don't use the key, it's a trap... I'm sorry, do not look back...

Tobias Jack Garner (12)
The Heath School, Runcorn

The End!

I looked around, desperately searching for an escape. Head-wrecking voices mumbled inside my head, demanding me to run. I didn't. Large trees caved me in, getting closer and closer. I looked around, but there was nothing. Was this going to be the end? He was coming. Fifty-three words left until the end... What was going to happen? Would I die? Would the world disappear? No one knew. The sky was getting closer, the ground was coming up. Only twenty words left... I heard him, he was coming. My heart was pounding. I could hear him coming. He was near me...

Alisha Buckley (12)
The Heath School, Runcorn

The Crazy Woods

"Don't go in the woods," they told me. "Some crazy things happen in there."

In the past, there had been stabbings, shootings and fights. Recently, kids had been going in, fighting after school, and then people recorded it and posted it on the Internet. Then the kids went viral. The police would go and inspect it, to see what was happening. The most recent incident was a man got shot in the head and then they were put under a load of leaves. The guy who'd shot him was arrested. It was why people called it The Crazy Woods...

Ryan Perry (15)
The Heath School, Runcorn

Endless!

Don't go in the woods, they told me... I was nowhere and I couldn't find my way out of the dark woods. I just heard the crickets and owls screaming their calls. I longed for daylight. I carried on walking, having that feeling of someone watching you, knowing you couldn't see them. In the distance was a distinct, huge hospital. However, it wasn't in this world, or the above. I entered. Suddenly, I turned a corner to see an asbestos sign dangling from the level above. Just then, I heard a strange sound whistling through the dark corridors...

Tom Radcliffe (13)
The Heath School, Runcorn

No Escape

I looked around, desperately searching for an escape. I got myself into this situation. I couldn't find anything, not even a hint. It was just me and him. Nervousness filled the room and chilled my spine. It was pitch-black. I could just about make out a table and chair where he'd sat, tapping his pen on the desk, which made this even more terrifying. I sat, silently waiting for him to say something. He opened a drawer and pulled out a gleaming knife. I instantly looked for an escape. There was nothing. I was doomed. I shrieked, "Help!"

Luke Hamilton (14)
The Heath School, Runcorn

Consequences

I knew there would be consequences, but I did it anyway. I had been dared by my friends to set off the school's fire alarms. I stood in front of the principal, my hands shaking. He finally spoke after a minute's silence.

"Why did you do it?" he said, a serious look on his face.

I muttered quietly, "Because I was dared to..."

He looked at me sternly, "By who?"

I didn't want to tell on my friends, so instead I said the first thing that came to my head.

"It was... It was just me."

Molly Jones (12)
The Heath School, Runcorn

Home

My torch flickered and went out, now I lay in the tight bunks watching the sky, telling myself I was at home not here, not lying here. It stank, rats everywhere, mud everywhere. The smell of old food and corpses overwhelmed my senses. Everyone coughed and spluttered, the sound of scuttling animals and the constant noise in my ears told me to go home. I often thought about home and how it was always bright: bright lights, bright clothes, just... bright. I loved the torch, I took it everywhere. When it went out, I thought, *why aren't I home?*

Martha McVey (14)
The Heath School, Runcorn

Stuck

I looked, desperately searching for an escape. I saw a brown, hollow door. Something echoed, "Get me out!"
It came from the other side. I yelled back, "Hello!"
But, as I shouted, it got hotter and hotter. There was no hope for me, I was stuck, alone. I sat in the dark, empty corner, dying from the extreme temperature rise. Water fell from my eyes, dripping down my face. I knew I couldn't sit there, relying on someone to save me, so I dragged my dead body off the floor and limped to the back window, where no one stood.

Mia Groves (14)
The Heath School, Runcorn

The Decision

"You can save only one," the voice said.

I needed no reminder, the decision had filled my head ever since I was first presented with it. Even eventual sleep didn't stop it. It filled my dreams just like my life and still I came no closer to making a decision. I simply couldn't. The scene that you'd expect to see in a film or nightmare had become a harsh reality for me and I couldn't simply say, "That'll never happen to me."

It was reality. In the final opportunity to make a decision, I had no choice...

Lewis Whitehead (14)
The Heath School, Runcorn

Followed

Don't go in the woods, they told me. I should've listened. I was now lost in this jungle and it was turning into night. There was nowhere to go, everywhere looked the same. The ghostly trees draped over me and scraped my head as I tried to duck. My hands were trembling. I couldn't keep still. I felt like I was being watched, like my every move was being tracked precisely. The branches underneath me snapped as I began to run. They echoed throughout the woods. My heart began to boom through my chest, but the echo wasn't from me...

Phoebe Kinsella (14)
The Heath School, Runcorn

Matches

I looked around, desperately searching for an escape, although it was practically impossible as the dirt from beneath me began to circle the air, slowly muffling my senses. I ran my hands down the sides of what seemed to be a small room and could feel a box beside my rickety boots. Optimistically, I presumed this would help me but, after tinkering with the box, I realised they were matches. Still, I lit one to regain my sense of sight and gasped in horror of what was before me. I didn't know why or how, but I'd been buried alive...

Katie Wadcock (14)
The Heath School, Runcorn

Life Or Death?

"You can only save one," the voice exclaimed.

It was hard to tell whether it was imaginary or reality, but this was reality. I was terrified. I was at gunpoint with my family, but I had one person I could save: my mum, my dad or my baby brother. It was the hardest decision of my life yet. Each had their own reason to be saved, but I really didn't know.

"Come on and hurry up!" the voice shouted.

I was at the point where tears were slowly moving down my face, this decision was between life or death!

Ben McShane (12)
The Heath School, Runcorn

The Stranger In The Night

"Don't go in the woods at night," they told me. "It is too dangerous for you."
I thought to myself for a minute, *what would happen if I went in there alone at the dead of night?*
"Charlie! Charlie! Is anybody in there?" they groaned.
A few hours scrambled by and finally everyone was asleep. I went into the dark, scary woods. It was cold, in fact, it was freezing. As I secretly travelled further into the woods, there was a person. He took me. Would I be able to escape or would I die?

Ella Duffy (12)
The Heath School, Runcorn

Demons Of The Dark

My torch flickered and went out. My hands were clammy as the lifeless torch tumbled towards the ground. My senses became disorientated as my body tried to comprehend what was happening. I froze, my body froze, but my mind didn't. All of a sudden, I was being yelled at, my demons were coming to life in front of me. My speech was strangling me as the demons continued their destructive scheme to make me feel like I was prey and they were predators after my life. I was no longer in control of my actions, the demons were, for now...

Emily Rose Shaw (14)
The Heath School, Runcorn

Pitch-Black

My torch flickered and went out. At that point, I knew I was alone. Everywhere I looked was pitch-black. I stood alone as I thought to myself, *where am I? What happened and what am I going to do?* Suddenly, my heart skipped a beat as I heard something drop to the floor, which meant only one thing: someone or something was coming for me. I tried to open the door, but no matter how hard I tried, the door would just not open. Footsteps grew closer. At that moment, I thought I was done for when suddenly... *crash!*

Keisha Handley (12)
The Heath School, Runcorn

Alone!

The torch flickered and went out. I was stood there in the dark with the wind howling and the trees rustling: no one was around. I was alone, isolated, lost. Nowhere to go, no help, no way out. The sad, sorrowing sight of the dull blackness of the night... an owl hooted and stalked me, his beady eyes gleamed at every step I took. The only light I saw was the shimmering pearl of the moon. Where was I? Would I ever get back home? The shivers rippled up my spine as I heard the branches snapping repeatedly... *Crash!*

Teighan Georgia Simpson (12)
The Heath School, Runcorn

Headlights!

My torch flickered and went out, on the coldest night of the year my tyre had burst. I could hear crackling noises coming from the woods, was it a creature of some sort? A white layer began to emerge on the road around me, at that moment I knew I was in trouble. As the night went on, noises from the woods got louder, but there was no sign of any civilisation. Headlights! Around the corner came a set of headlights, was this the hope that was going to get me home? The car came to an abrupt stop.
"Hello...?"

Leah Challoner (14)
The Heath School, Runcorn

Uncle, Oh Uncle

I looked around, desperately searching for an escape.
"Hey, little boy. Why would you hide from Uncle Resnov?"
His intentions were clear, to seek me and sell me as a slave. My heartbeat played a song in my chest. My eyes darted around the room, looking for a way out. My legs felt like jelly. I was like a sore thumb: I stuck out. A breeze, I covered my mouth and there he was, glaring at a dark corner where I happened to be. I ran with every bit of energy, then it all came down. The exit was there...

Owen Jamie Davidson (16)
The Heath School, Runcorn

The Bridge

"You can save only one," the voice said.
My blindfold was then taken off. I was expecting the worst, yet what I saw was beautiful. I was stood on a huge bridge surrounded by nature, then I heard screaming. My name. I looked down to the floor beneath the bridge and my younger twin sisters and my younger brother were all hanging from the bridge by a rope. I took one and held it, the others fell. I didn't see who'd survived, but then I heard my sister scream. She was still hanging from the bridge.

Olivia Dutton (14)
The Heath School, Runcorn

Lost

My torch flickered and went out...

At this point, I was starting to panic. It was a rainy, cold night and I was abandoned in the woods, trying to find shelter or a place to stay, but I couldn't think straight. I had a constant worry that a wild animal would attack me. I would be defenceless with no way to fight back or even see where I was heading. I slowly started to realise that I wasn't getting home anytime soon, even though it made me feel scared inside. I realised I had to overcome my fear, this would be the time I took responsibility...

Michael Lavelle (14)
The Heath School, Runcorn

The Door

The door creaked open. The mysterious, eerie shadows I could see through the door made me think again about this mission. The voices in my head told me not to go in, but my shivering legs stumbled towards the brown, wooden door. My hand nervously grabbed the shining, gold handle. It made a screeching sound as I twisted it. The door slowly opened. Behind the door was darkness, nothing but darkness. I could hear my heart beating in my chest as fast as a cheetah while taking my first step into the unknown darkness...

Emily Barrett (12)
The Heath School, Runcorn

The Darkness And Me

My torch flickered and went out. Now there was nothing but the darkness and me. The leaves crunched and branches snapped, I questioned if I was alone. Something caught my arm and pulled me down to the ground. I scrambled for the nearest tree trunk, holding on for my life. Just as a sense of hope filled me, it was taken away when it grabbed my feet and pulled me down to the ground again, the rough bark cutting my hands. I crawled away, managing to get to my feet, and ran as quickly as I could towards the darkness.

Paige O'Neill (14)
The Heath School, Runcorn

Idolish7

Inspired by Uta No Prince-Sama

Please let this be a dream, I thought to myself as a crowd of fans cheered us on, singing our favourite song: 1000% Love! Our group, Idolish7, were under too much pressure seeing as this was only our second time performing on stage and we already had 3,000 fans watching us. Although it was awesome that we had so many fans, it was just too much for us. As we got off the stage, we all gasped for air as if we were being strangled to death. In front of us was our composer, smiling from cheek to cheek.

Lilly Bang (12)
The Heath School, Runcorn

Light

My torch flickered and went out. The only source of protection and security I had just went in an instant. I tried to hold my heavy breaths, but the eeriness was too much. Reality had become a blur at this point. I didn't know where I was headed, what I was feeling, but I felt lost and wanted to escape. I could feel the presence of what seemed like 100 people isolating me and breathing on the hairs of my neck. I knew it was in my head, but I knew for sure that the hand on my shoulder wasn't...

Kyle Mainwaring (14)
The Heath School, Runcorn

The Bang

My torch flickered and went out. I couldn't see a thing, the dark aura surrounded me. I was petrified. I could feel and hear the spirits fly around me. I was getting very worried now, my bones started to tingle and freeze. I could hear footsteps coming up the stairs at a rapid pace. The door slammed and my heart sank, tears came flying down my face. I started to scream as loudly as I could at the top of my lungs. I ran to the window, opened it and, as quickly as I could, I climbed down safely.

Joseph Butler (15)
The Heath School, Runcorn

Hangman

Don't go in the woods, my friend told me. I was curious now he'd told me not to go in the woods. I thought to myself, *what could be in there? Could there be a chest, a gun or even a briefcase full of money?*
A day later, I went into the dark, creepy woods and, as soon as I went in, I saw something glowing right in the middle of all the trees. I approached the glowing object cautiously and, as I got there, I saw a person hanging from a rope tied tightly around their neck...

Callum Evans (13)
The Heath School, Runcorn

Zombies

My torch flickered and went out. The cave was now in complete darkness. I walked forwards and hit my head on a rock. I was dizzy, I could see the light at the end of a cave. Out of nowhere, a terrifying zombie came out of a shadow and attacked me. I used my only weapon (my torch) and struck the horrifying zombie in the head. The cave was like a maze. I couldn't find a way out, I could hear a low, constant, buzzing noise which fortunately led me to the end of the cave. I was so relieved.

Harvey Coughlan (12)
The Heath School, Runcorn

The Woods

A long time ago, I was in the woods looking for my dog. I heard leaves crunch behind me. I carried on walking and just ignored it. Then I heard a voice shouting, "Ben! Help!" The voice sounded like my dad. I got my phone out and rang my dad, he didn't pick up. I heard his ringtone, it sounded like it was coming from the trees. I called my mum, but she didn't pick up either so I just carried on walking, shouting for my dog. I suddenly felt something hard on my face...

Aaron Lee Smith (12)
The Heath School, Runcorn

The Claw

I entered the room in shock, the room where the murder scene took place. The lights flickered in the room of silence. The door slammed in the room of torture. A loud bang hit the floor demandingly. The room was getting shallower and shallower by the moment. All I saw was a large claw above me. I hoped it was a dream until the sharp claw stabbed me. I looked around the room for an escape, there was nothing. Was it a trap? It picked me up as if I was its enemy and threw me into the darkness.

Jessica Daci (12)
The Heath School, Runcorn

In The Night Garden

Don't go in the woods, they told me. I did it anyway. It was late and I never dropped out of a dare. It was Friday the thirteenth and it was 2.23am. I sneaked out the house at midnight and had been playing out since then. We got bored, so we started playing truth or dare at 2.15. It got harder and harder the more we played. I nearly asked to stop playing when it was my turn. I picked dare and my friend thought for about a minute. He told me to go into the deep, dark, eerie woods.

Oliver Kinsella (12)
The Heath School, Runcorn

Who Should I Revive?

"You can only save one," the voice said.
It was either Leah Davise or Ethan Davise and Leah had RPGs and Ethan had a SCAR, a heavy shotgun and an RPG. He had the three good guns and he was also the best player, so I would need him to help me get the Victory Royale. Leah had two kills, Ethan had four and I had nine kills, but I needed to kill the people who killed them. I was only on two HP. As I was reviving Ethan, I heard the storm and it killed all three of us...

James Walsh (12)
The Heath School, Runcorn

The Oblation

"You can save only one," the voice said.
Who should I choose? My two life-long lovers, I didn't know who to choose. I still loved both men standing before me, hanging in chains.
"Stop! I can't do it. How could I save them both? I must save them, please."
"You can, but you must do something in return," he snarled.
"Fine, just let them go!" I cried.
"Then it is time for your oblation," he snarled...

Elle Louise Edwards (12)
The Heath School, Runcorn

The Woods

Don't go in the woods, they told me, but I had to disobey it. As I stealthed out of my house, I walked into the woods. A mile in, there was a snap of a branch. I stopped dead. I slowly turned to a pair of red eyes. They started multiplying into hundreds of red eyes. They circled me. I ran through the last gap I could see, past the scary figures. I ran and ran. I got to the sudden edge, ran to the street and into my house where my family were.
"You were right!"

Oliver Slama (12)
The Heath School, Runcorn

Please Let This Be A Dream, I Thought...

There was so much to do, but little time to do it. I needed to escape this cell (the old basement), I'd been trapped here ever since I'd heard a noise in the old, haunted basement. It was only a squirrel searching for food. It disappeared and the stairs creaked as I walked up them. The creaking made me nervous and the metal door slammed shut. It locked me in. The stairs collapsed beneath me. I was trapped in the basement. The walls closed in. I had to escape...

Jayme Robert-Lee Chadwick (12)
The Heath School, Runcorn

The Entrance

The floorboards creaked as I progressed, then something blasted me into a wall. I woke up to find myself hanging from the wall, nails attaching me. I saw a group of clowns with knives staring at me. I grabbed the gun from the waistband of my trousers and fired. A clown dropped as I shot. One by one, they fell until there were none left. I wriggled free from the nails and ran. I ran into an empty room. I was safe. I saw a dark figure approach as I slammed the door shut.

John James Hough (12)
The Heath School, Runcorn

Falling

"You can only save one," the voice said.
The voice awoke the silence that needed to be broken. Was this real? It sure felt like it and I wished it was a dream. I had always been told I wished and dreamt too much. I'd been disrespected my whole life, so why should I be saved? Lola liked Tiffany more than me, it was obvious. I had nothing but negativity brought to me and I was sick of it!
"Save her!"
She let go of my hand...

Sadie Lewtas (12)
The Heath School, Runcorn

The Shadow

Don't go in the woods, they told me as I was looking straight through the dark, gloomy woods. I asked myself what was in there, was it a bear? Was it a wolf? Or was it a murderer? I took a step and I saw something move, what was it? Its shadow was large and dark. I had the shivers. I couldn't move, my feet were stuck to the ground; was it coming to get me? I had five minutes left. I could see it... I ran.

Mason McIntyre (12)
The Heath School, Runcorn

Hostage Situation

"You can save only one," the voice said.
It was right, there was no time to save two. She may be ace in her field of work, but the pressure was too immense at gunpoint to pick and save a life.
"Pick now!" the voice bellowed.
Time was slipping through her hands like sand with the victims both bleeding out. However, she couldn't choose to pick one over the other.
"Okay! Okay... I choose..."
Looking at the shaded figure, "Gareth!" the other victim cried out in despair, searching for mercy. Then she got to work with a knife.

Rooshy Patel (13)
West Hill School, Thompson Cross

The Hitroshmu Shing Forest

Don't go into the woods, they told me. I should've listened. The Hitroshmu Shing forest was invaded in 2013 after a political outburst started. I'd entered, uneasily through the dingy entrance. The sign said, *Military Only. Anyone Found Will Receive The Death Penalty.* If I was found, all I had to protect myself was a baton. Although I knew the consequences, I wandered in. Four men approached me in a circle, all with their assault rifles aimed at my head. The man in front of me had a smile spread from cheek to cheek. One bullet and I was dead.

Samuel Potts (13)
West Hill School, Thompson Cross

Fury Of Death!

Don't go in the woods, they told me, but did I listen? No. Yet still I plundered amongst the deafening shrieks and then, emerging from the death-stricken, intertwined tentacles of impenetrable sorrow, was a pale, yellow-eyed fury. A blade was hurled, lurching into the morbid abyss of darkness and the only colour observable was a dark red soup, puddling in fragmented pieces.
"The cold..." I muttered in a light voice.
A haunting breath lingered, embosoming my sorrowful body. Don't go in the woods, they told me, but did I listen? No.

Charlie Henry Stafford (13)
West Hill School, Thompson Cross

The Scream Of Death

I looked around, desperately searching for an escape, but the wall was too high for my short, stubby fingers to grasp. A searchlight flooded the room with a glow like the summer sun as the pulsating cry of the siren stopped echoing throughout the streets. I spotted a wooden chair underneath a layer of fallen plaster and rubble and perched myself on top of the wooden back of the seat with my unsteady feet. I let out a cry for help as a man with a flat-rimmed tin hat approached me hastily as the siren screamed to life again...

Thomas Whitfield (13)

West Hill School, Thompson Cross

The Escape

I looked around, desperately searching for an escape. It was so hard because it was a blackout. I could feel the lava rising below my feet. Suddenly, some rocks went flying high above my head and then the cave lit up with steaming, hot lava. I tried to run away but it moved at a high speed. I felt as though I was in quicksand. I thought there could be an exit where the lava had come from, so I jumped and grabbed the rock above me. I climbed over the lava and fell. It was just a black hole...

Owen Hague (13)
West Hill School, Thompson Cross

Evan Demon: The Voices

"Tell me everything you know, child," the female voice asked Evan Demon.

He shrank back into the van.

"Murder," said the voices in Evan's head.

He beamed an inferno from his eyes at the gas tank.

Kaboom! went the voices.

"Death can't be fooled," said Death (the female voice).

The fire wouldn't burn the black, obsidian dashboard. Evan couldn't die, he was immortal and a demon.

"You are the one in the prophecy, the one who can grant immortality to mortals," Death announced. "You are life, my enemy."

Evan was stunned and barely spoke, "I am the All Powerful One."

Fergus McGlone (12)
William Howard School, Brampton

The Maze Of Disappearance...

I looked around, desperately searching for an escape. I thought entering this maze competition (The Maze of Disappearance) would be fun, but turns out, it wasn't. I entered full of energy, desperate to find the missing diamond, running around the dark, creepy corners, ducking under the branches that were trying to kill me. I thought I was progressing through this mess, but it turned out that I wasn't. I felt like I was going for hours on end but then, out of the corner of my eye, I glimpsed the prettiest, most beautiful diamond, sparkling like one thousand galaxies.

Lucy Tait (12)
William Howard School, Brampton

No Way Out

I looked around, searching desperately for an escape. Around me, narrow mirrors were surrounding me. I looked up, I was drawn to my figure reflecting from the mirror. Looking in every direction, I stared blankly towards the mirrors. My hands were shaking, my mouth went dry, I was unsure of what to do. Spinning around hysterically, I was seeking for an escape. Would this be the end? Was there an escape? Would I survive? Unexpectedly, the light surrounding me flickered. Breathing heavily, I gave up on hope. It was unbearable, there was no way out. I would be there forever...

Sarah Jane Cochrane (12)
William Howard School, Brampton

The Old Abandoned House

Keep Out! Danger! The signs said around the old fence. They kept all intruders out. Rumours spread about spirits trapped inside. Nobody knew who they were, why they were there, millions of questions, yet no answers. Maggie didn't fit in at her school. See, she was an orphan, her family didn't know why she was different either, but they still loved her. In the afternoon, Maggie went down to an old house she'd never seen before. It felt familiar somehow. The signs told her to go away, but she stayed. This house was to unravel her biggest secret yet...

Rosie McCormick (11)
William Howard School, Brampton

Mystery Man

My torch flickered and went out. I looked around, desperately searching for an escape, but I couldn't find one. Where was I? I could hear the leaves around me rustling.
"Hello," said a deep, dark voice. "I am here to give you what you desire, and what you desire is so precious."
I could feel my heart pounding as if there was a thunderstorm inside me. Suddenly, the ground cracked underneath me. I fell down through the ground and through all of my memories. *Crash!* I landed back on my bed. I was alive! I had escaped! I was safe!

Antonia Kirkpatrick (12)
William Howard School, Brampton

Prisoner

My face plunged into water, cold as ice, chilling me to the bone. I gasped, desperate for air. Painfully, the hooded men yanked my head out of the bucket. I relished the air entering my lungs. Then the biggest, strongest man turned his head and pulled out a gun from his hoodie, frayed in places. I shivered as he pointed the gun at my face. He said, "Tell me everything you know, child."
"Nothing!" I replied quietly, still dazed from the lack of oxygen.
The man thrust the gun at my head. Pain exploded in my head. Everything went black...

Finlay Smith (12)
William Howard School, Brampton

They Told Me

Don't go in the woods, they told me. Lonely, I stood, the leaves crunched with every step. I heard mumbling from the edge of the woods, it was a man's voice, deep and rough. He shouted, "Help! Come to me!"

I couldn't resist following his scratchy voice. I walked closer, I saw a tall figure standing by a tree. I looked at him, he looked at me.

"Hello Michael," he said.

I was terrified, who was this man? Why did he know me? I began to run, he ran after me. Don't talk to strangers, they told me.

Katie Barclay (12)
William Howard School, Brampton

From Beyond The Grave

Today, I hired someone to solve my murder. It wasn't so much a person as a thing. It was from the realm beyond, from the other side. I didn't remember much about my last moments other than the pain and the blood. There was so much of that crimson liquid seeping out of me, a pool accumulated around my feet. When I finally passed through the veil, I called for him. He came, parting the onslaught of spirits, speeding towards me. He listened, he thought and then he left. He would bring me justice. My killer would be apprehended.

Zachary Ealey (12)
William Howard School, Brampton

The Compound (A Comedy)

The sign read, *Danger! Keep Out!* I got out my wooden, razor-sharp scissors. They were wooden so I didn't get cooked inside out from the high voltage that surged through the barrier between me and my goal. The flies in the cold, night air were zapped as they flew into the fence, sending static through my body, electrifying hairs on it. I crept through certain death (which was the fence) and made my way through the high, green grass. I entered the compound, round corners I sneaked. I could hear my heart in my chest...

Lewis Turner (11)
William Howard School, Brampton

Night Howlers

Silently, night fell and I was all alone in my little home as my mam and dad were not in sight.
"Don't go in the woods," they told me as they slammed the back door.
The veins in my body tightened. I heard screams from the Night Howlers, tweeting from the birds. I was alone. I packed my new bag and ran down the stairs. I walked out the back door, I was outside now. In the woods, I walked ahead, I didn't know what was waiting for me. Twigs crackled, owls hooted, no turning back now. I was stuck.

Darcie Dixon (12)
William Howard School, Brampton

Insane

I looked around, desperately searching for an escape. Rummaging around the bushes, approaching quietly, I dashed the other way, moving on my feet, dodging tree trunks and stones. The trees started to fade and the stars lit the sky in the night. I ran, then froze. *Creak* was the noise behind me as I looked out to the night, my back facing the wood. Lights like the sun shone in my eye. I stepped back. "No," said the voice in pain and the wind picked up behind me.

I felt nothing from then on.

Rebecca Illidge (12)

William Howard School, Brampton

What An Amazing Escape!

I looked around, desperately searching for an escape. Why was I in prison? What had I done wrong? It was really warm in my prison cell. It was like a warm, summer's day. The judge was ready to find out whether I was guilty or not.
"Guilty."
I had to make up a plan to make an escape. How could I get away? I could escape through the top of my prison cell? I needed to make contact with someone so that they could try and help me escape. However, there was an electrical fence. What could I do now?

Heathcliff Stone (12)
William Howard School, Brampton

Dark Escape

I searched round, desperately looking for an escape but all I could see was bodies. Most had rotted to the bone, starved, tortured. I wished I never went into the dark woods. Every time I thought of being taken from the woods by the stranger, goosebumps went up like a firework. I couldn't bear to live with the bodies staring at me. As I searched, I found a loose plank on the floor. I lifted it up and found my final escape. It was a dark tunnel. I wandered on to find out where it led to...

Harry Macnaughton (12)
William Howard School, Brampton

The Statue

Don't go in the woods, they told me. I knew they had, but I did it anyway. I lay there, silent, alone, or so I thought... I turned around wearily. I knew it was there, it'd followed me. I knew the idea was in my head, or was it? I woke up there, in the centre of a clearing, once again, alone and silent. I stood up and saw it, nothing, not at all. I thought to myself, *who am I? Should I just stay here?* I stood there, stone-like, stable, secure, forever...

Ewan Dearman (12)
William Howard School, Brampton

YOUNG WRITERS INFORMATION

We hope you have enjoyed reading this book – and that you will continue to in the coming years.

If you're a young writer who enjoys reading and creative writing, or the parent of an enthusiastic poet or story writer, do visit our website **www.youngwriters.co.uk**. Here you will find free competitions, workshops and games, as well as recommended reads, a poetry glossary and our blog.

If you would like to order further copies of this book, or any of our other titles, then please give us a call or visit **www.youngwriters.co.uk**.

Young Writers
Remus House
Coltsfoot Drive
Peterborough
PE2 9BF
(01733) 890066
info@youngwriters.co.uk

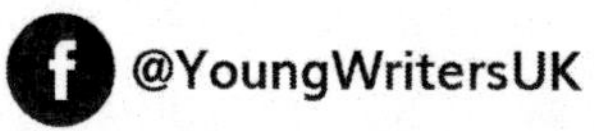